Written by Jenna Harmke
Artwork by Jenna Harmke and Toby Mikle

Today is my first day of
preschool and I am so excited!

I put on my favorite pink dress for this very special day.

Mommy made me chocolate chip smiley face pancakes with a whipped cream nose for breakfast.

Then we got in the car and
drove to school!

After I got out of the car,
I gave Mommy a big hug.

I walked into my classroom...
And it was HUGE!!!

We all sat around a big table
and drew a picture of our families.

While I was drawing, another bunny in my class tapped on my shoulder.

Then she just walked away.

I was so embarrassed.

Why couldn't I hear
what she was saying?

The school day ended.
Mommy came and picked me up.

Mommy said she was going to
take me to a special doctor
to see if they can fix it.

This place was called the
ear doctor.

I played a bunch of games with the doctor and when I was done, the doctor told me I needed hearing aids.

"Hearing aids will help you hear better!"
the doctor said

"I want those!" I exclaimed.
Everyone laughed.

It gets even better... I got
to pick the color I wanted!

I picked PINK!

When I put them in my ears,
I could hear so many new sounds.

It was crazy!!

The next day at school, I could hear all my friends when they talked to me and I didn't say "what" once.

I love my new hearing aids!

Thanks for reading!

Jenna Harmke
Original Artwork

Then we got in the car and drove to school!

Today is my first day of preschool and I am so excited!

"Bessie Needs Hearing Aids" is a children's book that will help children with hearing loss understand the process, and that they are not alone. Written and illustrated by a teenage girl who went through this process, so it will resonate with children just learning of hearing issues, or coping with wearing hearing aids. The book received numerous accolades so it was decided to make it available to all, in order to possibly help other children with hearing loss.

17744674R00017